This book belongs to

To Mum & Joe
for their inspiration
M.M.

First published in Great Britain in 2006 by Gullane Children's Books
This paperback edition published in 2007 by
Gullane Children's Books
an imprint of Pinwheel Limited

Winchester House, 259-269 Old Marylebone Road,
London NW1 5XJ

1 3 5 7 9 10 8 6 4 2

A CIP record for this title is available from the British Library.

ISBN-10: 1-86233-674-1
ISBN-13: 978-1-86233-674-2

Printed and bound in China

Little Lion Lost!

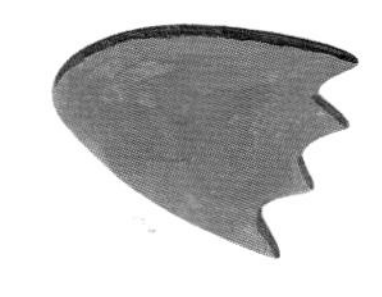

Mark Marshall

Little Lion was playing in the warm afternoon sun.

He especially loved to chase frogs!

But Little Lion ran too far into the jungle,
and he soon realised he was lost and alone.
He looked around and spotted some footprints.
They could be my mum's, thought Little Lion.

And he scampered on until the
footprints led him to . . .

...Crocodile.

"Hello, Crocodile. Have you seen my mum?" asked Little Lion.

"No, I haven't seen her," snapped Crocodile, "but I will help you look."

With a splash and a mighty
flick of his tail, crocodile was gone.
"Wait," spluttered Little Lion, "I can't swim!"

Alone again, Little Lion decided to follow a new set of footprints. *Wow, I can fit all of my paws in one of these!* he thought.

The enormous prints led him to . . .

...Elephant.

"Hello, Elephant. Have you seen
my mum?" asked Little Lion.
"No, I haven't seen her," she trumpeted,
"but I will help you look."

The ground shook as Elephant charged off.

"Wait for me!" panted Little Lion, but he couldn't keep up with Elephant's huge strides.

Alone again, he decided to
follow a new set of footprints.
This time they led him to . . .

"Hello, Monkey!" called Little Lion.
"Have you seen my mum?"
"No, I haven't seen her," he
chattered, "but I will help you look."

With a loud rustle, Monkey swung
though the tree-tops and disappeared.
"Wait, Monkey," Little Lion shouted,
"I don't think I can climb this tree!"

Alone again, Little Lion wished he could find his mum's footprints.

Crocodile's were webbed.
Elephant's were just ENORMOUS.
And Monkey's were far too long and thin!

Where can she be?

"I think it's time to go home,"
Said a familiar voice.
Little Lion span round to see . . .

. . . Mummy!
"I've been looking everywhere for you,"
he purred, "how did you find me?"
"Well, that's simple," she said,
"I followed *your* footprints!"

Little Lion sat on his mum's back
and together they followed their
footprints all the way home.

other Gullane children's Books for you to enjoy . . .

Brown Bear's Wonderful Secret
CAROLINE CASTLE
TINA MACNAUGHTON

New Kid in Town
CLAIRE FREEDMAN
KRISTINA STEPHENSON

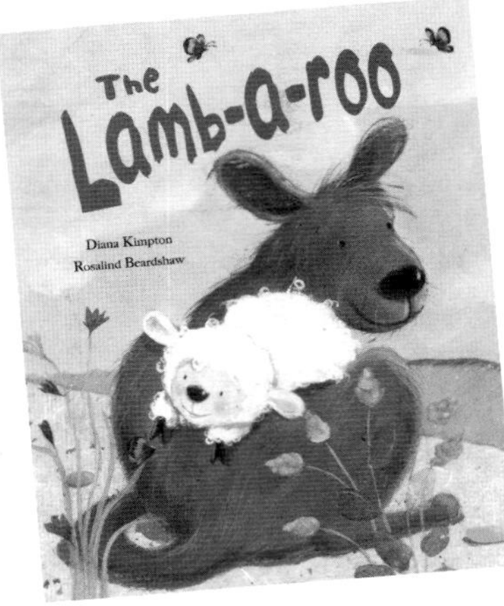

The Lamb-a-roo
DIANA KIMPTON
ROSALIND BEARDSHAW

Rocky and the Lamb
GREG GORMLEY
LYNNE CHAPMAN